Bibi

Jo Weaver

Hodder
Children's
Books

On a still morning the sun rose over the lake.
Bibi ruffled her feathers and opened an eye.
She had been with the flock for as long as anyone
could remember, and was older than anyone knew.

Her name could often be heard amid the chatter on the lake.

"Bibi showed me how to preen my feathers."

"Bibi taught me how to stand on one leg."

Every flamingo recognised her call, as she guided them in a graceful dance on the glassy water.

When new parents were ready
to lay their eggs, Bibi led them away
from the edge of the lake. There on
the soft mud, she showed them how
to build nests for their chicks.

"Welcome to the flock, Toto," she
said, greeting the newest flamingo.

The chicks took their first steps here, growing stronger every day.
But as the sun beat down, the earth around them was drying up quickly.

"We can't stay here any longer," the flamingos agreed.
"There's no food, no shade . . ."

"No water!" said Bibi, turning towards the lake.

The water's edge had shrunk away, into the shadow of the distant volcano.
They could reach it quickly by air, but their chicks couldn't fly yet.

"I know the way by foot," said Bibi to the flamingos. "You fly ahead, and I'll walk with your chicks. We'll meet you by the shore."

"How do you know where to go?" the chicks asked Bibi anxiously.

"I made this journey when I was small like you.
I was afraid then too," she said.

As she spoke, she noticed a
small chick lagging behind.

It was Toto, collapsed on the dry
earth, exhausted by the heat.

"Keep moving, Toto!" the chicks called out.
"We want to get to the lake!"

Bibi gathered them into the shade of her wings.
"We'll rest with Toto for a while," she said, "until
we are all strong enough to continue together."

Whilst they waited, she told them about life on the lake.

Her stories of cool waters and fresh food gave Toto strength.
When he was ready, they all set off again.

"You stay beside me," Bibi told him.

On and on and on they walked,
across the scorching desert.

The shimmering outline of the volcano was slowly getting nearer, and at last they saw a sliver of silver glistening below it.

"I can see the lake!" Toto called out.

The chicks felt
damp earth beneath
their feet. Soon they
were splashing through
the cool water to join
their grateful parents.

For the rest of the summer, Bibi watched happily
as the chicks grew, their feathers turning
pink and readying for flight.

But she had begun to
feel tired and old.

She knew that once the chicks could fly, the flock would move on. Bibi worried that she might not be strong enough to join them this time.

She slipped quietly away by herself.

Soon it was time for the flamingos to leave.

"Where is Bibi?" asked Toto.

Thousands of eyes searched the lake for their old friend.

"I see her!" Toto called. "She's lying on the shore."

The flamingos helped Bibi to stand.
"Let's clean off this sand," said one flamingo,
softly preening her feathers.

"Come back to the lake and eat with us,"
said another, leading her gently into the water.

"We'll all wait until you feel strong
enough to fly," said Toto.

Bibi ate and rested. Slowly, slowly, she gathered her strength,
and at last she was ready.

One by one, the flamingos took to the sky, until it was Bibi's turn to try.

She whispered one last goodbye to the lake,
stretched out her wings and ran . . .

... and she flew!

For Cath, for Nan, for Sheila.
And for my own Granny Mayhew.

HODDER CHILDREN'S BOOKS

First published in Great Britain in 2022 by Hodder & Stoughton

1 3 5 7 9 10 8 6 4 2

Text and illustrations copyright © Jo Weaver 2022

HB ISBN: 978 1 444 94871 4
PB ISBN: 978 1 444 94872 1

Printed and bound in China

Hodder Children's Books. An imprint of Hachette Children's Group. Part of Hodder & Stoughton
Carmelite House, 50 Victoria Embankment, London, EC4Y 0DZ

An Hachette UK Company
www.hachette.co.uk

www.hachettechildrens.co.uk